# The Wheels on the Bus

*To Alice Kovalski*

First U.S. Edition

Musical Notation by Miriam Katzin

First Published in Canada by Kids Can Press

*Library of Congress Cataloging-in-Publication Data*

Kovalski, Maryann.
    The wheels on the bus.
    Summary: While a grandmother and grandchildren wait for the bus, they sing the title song with such gusto they miss their bus.
    1. Children's song — Texts. [I. Buses — Songs and music. 2. Songs] I. Title.
PZ8.3.K8535Wh  1987  [E]  87-3441
ISBN 0-316-50256-1 (hc)
ISBN 0-316-50259-6 (pb)

PB: 20 19 18 17 16 15 14 13

Printed in Hong Kong

# Maryann Kovalski

# The Wheels on the Bus

Little, Brown and Company
Boston  New York  Toronto  London

One day, Grandma took Jenny and Joanna shopping for new winter coats.

They tried on long coats and short coats, blue coats and red coats, plaid coats and even raincoats. Joanna chose a coat with wooden barrel buttons. Jenny liked it too, because of the hood.

When it was time to go home, the bus didn't come for a long time and everyone grew tired. "I have an idea, sweeties," said Grandma. "Let's sing a song my Granny sang with u. when I was a little girl." And so they h to sing. . . .

The wipers on the bus go swish, swish, swish

swish, swish, swish

swish, swish, swish

The wipers on the bus go swish, swish, swish

all around the town.

The people on the bus hop on and off

on and off

on and off

The people on the bus hop on and off

all around the town.

The horn on the bus goes toot, toot, toot

toot, toot, toot

toot, toot, toot

The horn on the bus goes toot, toot, toot

all around the town.

The money on the bus goes clink, clink, clink

clink, clink, clink

clink, clink, clink

The money on the bus goes clink, clink, clink

all around the town.

The people on the bus go up and down

up and down

up and down

The people on the bus go up and down

all around the town.

The babies on the bus go waaa, waaa, waaa

waaa, waaa, waaa

waaa, waaa, waaa

The babies on the bus go waaa, waaa, waaa

all around the town.

The parents on the bus go ssh, ssh, ssh

ssh, ssh, ssh

ssh, ssh, ssh

The parents on the bus go ssh, ssh, ssh

all around the town.

The wheels on the bus go round and round

round and round

round and round

The wheels on the bus go round and round

all around the town.

Grandma, Jenny, and Joanna had so much fun . . .

They missed the bus!

So . . .

They took a taxi.